MOODY COW MEDITATES

Kerry Lee MacLean

Wisdom

Wisdom Publications
199 Elm Street
Somerville MA 02144 USA
wisdompubs.org

Text and illustrations © 2009 Kerry Lee MacLean,
kerryleemaclean.com

Library of Congress Cataloging-in-Publication Data
MacLean, Kerry Lee.
 Moody Cow meditates / Kerry Lee MacLean.
     p. cm.
 ISBN 0-86171-573-X (hardcover : alk. paper)
 1. Meditation—Juvenile fiction. I. Title.
 PZ10.3.M1983Mo 2009
 [E]—dc22
                           2009006556

ISBN 978-0-86171-573-2
eBook 978-0-86171-994-5

20 19 18 17 16
10   9   8   7

Cover design by Kerry Lee MacLean and Tony Lulek.
Interior design by Gopa&Ted2, with JB&LC.
Set in Cantoria 14/22.

Wisdom Publications' books are printed on acid-free paper
and meet the guidelines for permanence and durability of
the Production Guidelines for Book Longevity of the Coun-
cil on Library Resources.

Printed in the PRC..

DAISY

KEEP OUT

*Dedicated to
the Dalai Lama,
who is dedicated
to all children*

A NOTE TO GROWN-UPS: Most children will take naturally to meditation if you find ways to make the activity warm, welcoming, and fun. Try to follow meditation with quality time together—snuggling, playing, sipping hot chocolate—even if just for a few minutes. This daily ritual can create a peaceful ground from which kindness and wisdom can naturally grow.

My name is Moody Cow. It used to
be Peter, but now it's Moody Cow.
It all started one stupid, rotten day
when everything went wrong.

First, I had a bad dream…

...a VERY bad dream, which involved
a giant three-eyed alien.

What a rotten way to wake up.

mom?

I wanted to find my mom
and tell her about the giant three-eyed alien—
but I couldn't find her *anywhere*.

So, I admit, I was in a bad mood to begin with. Then, I couldn't find my skateboard. Turned out my sister had "borrowed" it.

"Daisy! Stop drawing on my skateboard!"

Okay, *maybe* I overreacted
when I pulled her tail—
but it *was* a brand-new
skateboard!

So then Daisy had to get me back
by tripping me on the stairs.

What a monster!

That made me mad—
so mad that I cut her doll's hair off.
On purpose.

Of course, I got in trouble for that—
which made me miss the bus!
I had to ride my bike all the way
to school… *in the snow*.

That made me *really* mad.

On the way
home from school
I hit a snow bank
and scraped my knee.

There was blood
everywhere!

The rest of the way,
I couldn't stop
thinking about how
my rotten day
was really Daisy's fault.
She put me in a bad mood
by drawing on my new skateboard.

"Ow! Ow! Ow!"

Or maybe it was the giant three-eyed alien's fault for giving me bad dreams. *Whatever.* I was so mad I couldn't see straight.

And when I turned into our driveway, I crashed right into my dad's truck.

Well, you can understand that with a bloody knee and a banged-up nose, I was madder than ever.

SUPER mad!

"Aahhhh!!! I can't take any more!"

And then I did something *crazy*.
I picked up my baseball
and threw it…
right through the window.
ON PURPOSE!

Unfortunately, my mom saw the whole thing.

"What on earth do you think you're doing?!" she yelled.
"Have you lost your mind?!"

She came outside, took one look at my super-mad, rotten-day face,
and I guess she felt sorry for me. "Aww... are you a little moody cow?"

Of course, my sister Daisy heard her say that.

She started shouting, *"Moody Cow! Moody Cow! Peter is a Moody Cow!"*

The next thing I knew, *all* the kids in the neighborhood joined in.

"We need Grandfather,"
Mom said, and picked up
the phone.

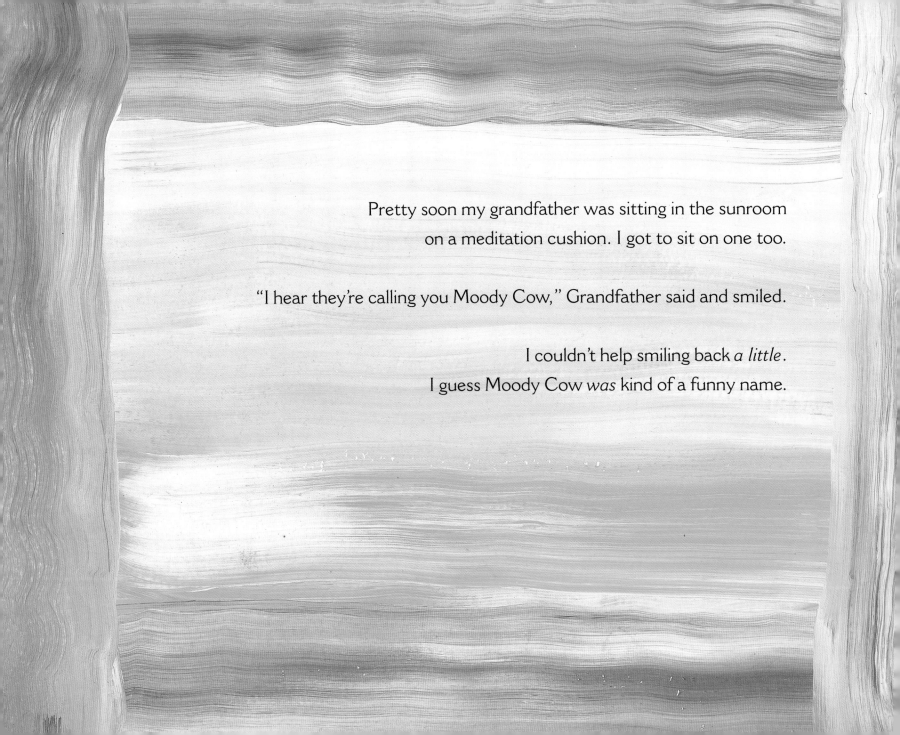

Pretty soon my grandfather was sitting in the sunroom
on a meditation cushion. I got to sit on one too.

"I hear they're calling you Moody Cow," Grandfather said and smiled.

I couldn't help smiling back *a little*.
I guess Moody Cow *was* kind of a funny name.

"See this?" he asked, as he pointed to a jar of water. "This is your mind," he said.

"And these," he held out a little dish of sparkles, "are your angry thoughts."

"*That*," I said, "is a jar of water, and *those* are Daisy's fairy dust sparkles."

"Come on, Mr. Moody Cow, work with me here. Now, what we're going to do is put in a pinch of sparkles for every angry thought you have. Then we're going to sit here until they all settle down to the bottom. By the time the water is clear again, your anger will have all settled down too."

"It won't work," I told him.

"Let's just see," he said.

I took a pinch of sparkles and
dropped it into the water.
"Which angry thought is that?"
Grandfather asked.
"That's the three-eyed alien.
It tried to gobble me up last night."
"Oh, I see. Rotten way to start
the day! Okay, what else?"
I put in another pinch for the next
angry thought. "This is me having
to clean the toilet for a *whole
month* for breaking the window.
I *hate* cleaning the toilet!"
"Me too. What else?"
I put in one more pinch of sparkles
and said, "This is Daisy drawing on
my *brand-new* skateboard with a
marker."
"Oh dear! She did that?"
Grandfather sighed, "Okay,
what else?"

"*This* pinch is when I missed the bus and had to ride my bike to school, *in the snow*."

"You can ride a bike through snow?" Grandfather asked.

"I have good tires."

"Anything else?"

"On my way home I scraped my knee and I was so mad I crashed into Dad's truck. I think I broke my nose!"

"Ouch!" Grandfather said. "That must have hurt."

"It did! *Then* I picked up my baseball and threw it through the window. *On purpose*."

"Wow! You should put in a *double* pinch for that one. I guess you really did have a Moody Cow day."

"I sure did!"

"Is that all?" Grandfather asked.

"Yeah... but it's *a lot!*"

"It sure is."

Grandfather put the lid on the jar and shook it up real good.

"This jar is like your mind right now," he said, "angry thoughts bouncing around all over the place."

"Now, let's see what happens when we let your angry thoughts settle down," Grandfather said, putting the Mind Jar down in front of me. "Just sit quietly and see what happens."

I sat up real straight, and then I got to ring the gong. *Bongggggg…*

I sat watching all my angry thoughts swirl around like crazy in the jar.

A few thoughts slowed down and sank to the bottom…
then a few more… and a few more…

It was so still I could feel my heart beating.
It was so quiet I could hear my breath going in… and out… in… and out…

I felt a ray of golden sunshine coming through the window.
It warmed my back and started to melt away the last of my anger.

Finally, Grandfather rang the gong to end the meditation. He leaned over to whisper in my ear. "Okay, this part's important. Don't move until you can't hear the sound of the gong anymore."

I cocked my head, listening closely. *Bongggggg*…
The ringing got softer… and softer… and softer… until I couldn't hear it at all.

Grandfather smiled and held up the jar. "Well, look at this! All the sparkles have settled down," he said.

"And my angry thoughts have, too!" I said. "I mean, I guess if I think about it, I *could* get mad again."

"That's probably true," he said. "But we had to work pretty hard to settle them down. Let's not stir them all up again!"

I laughed, for the first time that day.

"That thing is *cool!*" I said. "Can I keep it?"

"Sure," said Grandfather. He smiled and handed me the jar and the dish of sparkles. "A few minutes each day helps keep the Moody Cow away!"

I laughed again. "Thanks, Grandfather! Can we do this again tomorrow?"

"Of course! Let's try to do this together every day."

I went to my room and put the Mind Jar by my bed…
just in case the three-eyed alien ever comes back.

Now it's been *two whole weeks*
and I haven't had *one* Moody Cow day.

But I've decided to keep the name anyway...

I kind of like it!

The end.

THE MOODY COW MIND JAR

Look for the Mind Jar for iPhone/iPad in the App Store. Or if you'd like to make your own Mind Jar, here's one way to do it (adult supervision is necessary). Start by making sure you have these items on hand:

- **Some kind of empty and clean glass jar**—not too big, about the size of large baby food jar or a spice container.

- **Sparkles or glitter in at least one color**—you can get glitter at a stationery or craft store. *(Tinier sparkles work a little better than larger ones, if you have the option.)*

- **A bottle of glycerin**—you can get this inexpensively at a craft store or a health food store, and also at most drug stores. *(Glycerin thickens the water and helps the sparkles fall more slowly.)*

- **Some liquid dish soap or hand soap**—clear and colorless soap works best. *(Soap helps lower the surface tension of the water so the sparkles don't just stay on the top.)*

Fill the jar three-fourths full with *warm* tap water.

Add glycerin, almost to the top—but not too close. Put in around four *drops* of liquid soap. Put the lid on tightly and shake the jar enough to dissolve the glycerin and soap in the warm water. Take the lid off the jar. Now you are ready to begin the meditation activity.

The water in the jar is your mind's natural state. Put in a pinch of glitter/sparkles for each thought you notice. If you have more than one color of glitter, you can use different colored sparkles for different kinds of thoughts. For instance, you can use one color for angry thoughts, one color for fearful thoughts, and another color for other kinds of thoughts.

When you're ready, put the lid on tightly and mix it all up by turning the jar upside-down then right-side-up five or six times. Now you can see all the sparkles spinning and rushing around— this is your upset or busy mind.

Set the jar down, and breathe in and out slowly. You can gently ring a gong or bell if you have one. Notice how the sparkles settle slowly down to the bottom—as they do that, let your thoughts settle too. When you're ready, ring the gong again—make sure you notice how the sound gets softer and softer before it disappears! Save the Mind Jar to shake up and use next time.